First published in the United States of America in 2006 by
Walker Publishing Company, Inc.
Distributed to the trade by Holtzbrinck Publishers

First published in Great Britain by HarperCollins Children's Books in 2005

For information about permission to reproduce selections from
this book, write to Permissions, Walker & Company,
104 Fifth Avenue, New York, New York 10011

Library of Congress Cataloging-in-Publication Data
Chichester Clark, Emma.
Melrose and Croc / Emma Chichester Clark.
p. cm.
Summary: A chance meeting turns to friendship for a lonely crocodile
and a companionless golden retriever who both arrive in the city at Christmas time.
ISBN-10: 0-8027-9597-8 • ISBN-13: 978-0-8027-9597-7 (hardcover)
ISBN-10: 0-8027-9598-6 • ISBN-13: 978-0-8027-9598-4 (reinforced)
[1. Friendship—Fiction. 2. Loneliness—Fiction. 3. Christmas—Fiction. 4. Golden retriever—Fiction. 5. Dogs—Fiction.
6. Crocodiles—Fiction.] I. Title.
PZ7.C5435Mc 2006   [E]—dc22   2006006556

Visit Walker & Company's Web site at www.walkeryoungreaders.com

Printed in China

2 4 6 8 10 9 7 5 3 1

Melrose and Croc
A Christmas to Remember

Emma Chichester Clark

Walker & Company
New York

One day before Christmas, a small green crocodile walked down a busy street carrying a suitcase. Not far away, a yellow dog named Melrose was opening his front door.

Little green Croc had come to the city to see
Santa Claus at the big department store.

He was so excited. He looked at the piece of paper again. It said:

"Come and meet **SANTA CLAUS** *at Sax and Dale's! Make your dreams come true!"*

"Tomorrow," thought Croc, "will be wonderful."

Melrose had also just arrived in town. He was decorating his new apartment. "I wish I had somebody to do this with," he said to himself. "I wish someone else could see this."

He looked at the box of Christmas tree decorations.

"I may as well put these away again," he thought.

"There's no point in having a tree just for me."

That night, as Melrose gazed at the view, he sighed.

"It's Christmas. I should be happy, but I feel sad."

Little green Croc looked out at the great
dark sea. He was too excited, even to sleep.

In the morning, Croc arrived at Sax and Dale's.

"Can you tell me the way to Santa Claus?" he asked.

"Oh, I'm afraid you've missed him," said the manager.

"He was here last week. He's out now. It *is* Christmas Eve."

Croc felt like crying, but he didn't want people to see.

"I'm hopeless," thought Croc. "I've got everything wrong . . . and now I'm soaked!" Little green Croc burst into tears. It didn't matter anymore.

Melrose hadn't seen Croc or the puddle. He was
still finding his way around town. "I wish I could
find a way to cheer up," he thought.

"And I wish I could find a friend," he sighed.

A lady was giving away surprise presents.

"For you to share." She smiled.

"Thank you," Melrose said sadly.

Croc found a place to get out of the snow.

"How foolish I was to come," he thought. A tear

dropped onto his suitcase. Then suddenly, he

heard music, lovely music. It rang through the

air, and he followed it . . .

Little green Croc forgot everything.

He whirled and twirled. He glided and slid.

Melrose was there, whirling, too. He flew faster
than light. He felt lighter than air.

"If only I could skate forever!" thought Melrose. "If only I could skate forever!" thought Croc. They swooped and looped. They zig-zagged left and right . . . faster and faster . . . until . . .

CRASH!

"OW!" cried Melrose.
"OH!" cried Croc.

"I'm so sorry!" gasped Croc.

"No, *I'm* sorry!" said Melrose. "Come on, let's go have some tea."

They sat and told each other everything.

" . . . and now Christmas is ruined," Croc finished.

Then Melrose had a brilliant idea.

"Come and spend Christmas with me!" he cried.

"We'll get a tree, and Santa Claus will come!"

Croc wiped the last tear off his nose.

"I'd love to do that," he said.

While Melrose cooked dinner, little green Croc
decorated the tree.

"Look!" cried Melrose. "I told you he'd come!
There he is!"

The next day was Christmas.

"All my dreams are coming true!" said Croc.

"Mine, too," said Melrose. "All I wanted was a friend, and I found you!"

"And I found *you*! Merry Christmas." Croc smiled.